This Walker book belongs to:

....

....

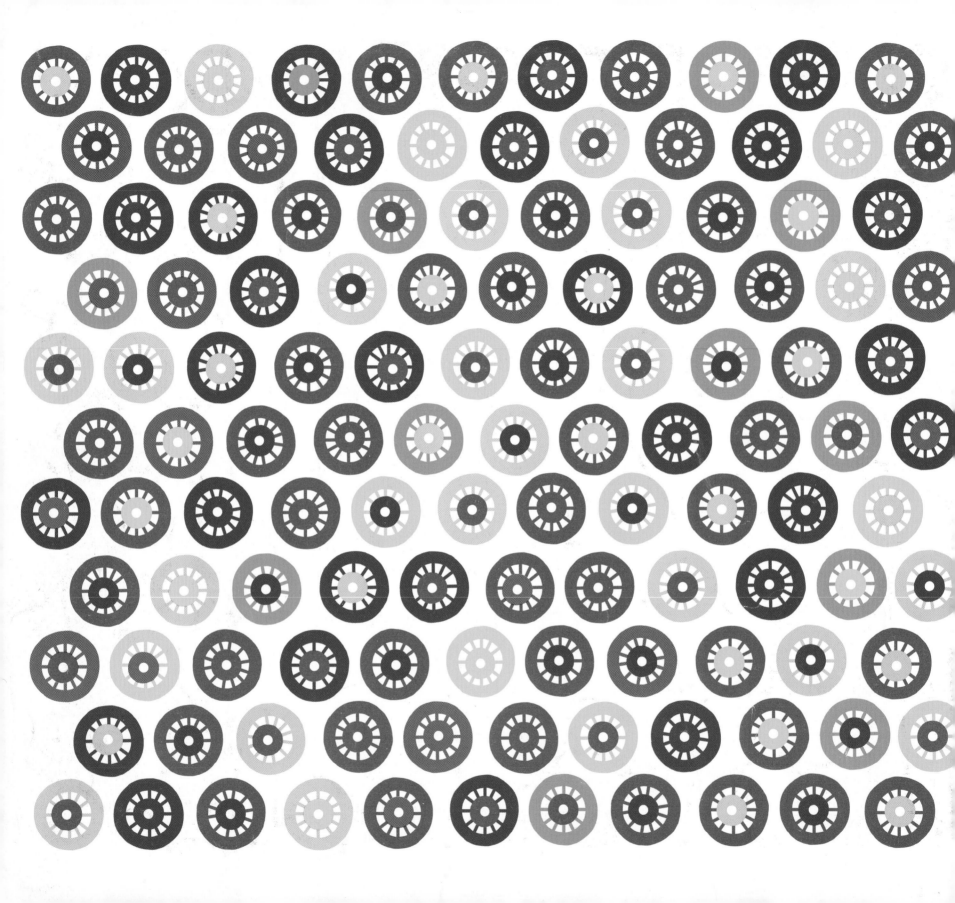

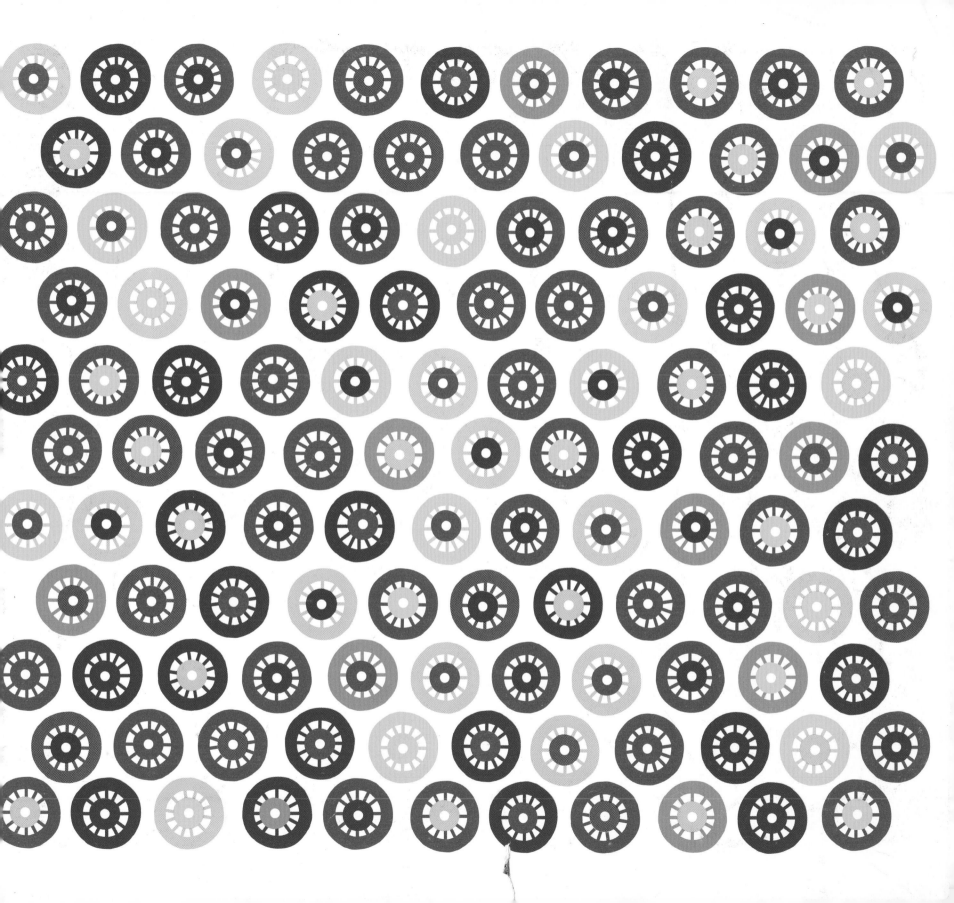

With thanks to my three guinea pigs . . .

Freddie, William and **Sam**

First published 2013 by Walker Books Ltd
87 Vauxhall Walk, London SE11 5HJ

This edition published 2014

10 9 8 7 6 5 4 3 2 1

This book has been typeset in Frutiger

Printed in China

British Library Cataloguing in Publication Data:
a catalogue record for this book is available from the British Library

ISBN 978-1-4063-5259-7

www.walker.co.uk

There are 15 snails in this book. Can you find all of them?

and the cars go...

william bee

WALKER BOOKS
AND SUBSIDIARIES
LONDON · BOSTON · SYDNEY · AUCKLAND

Here is the policeman off on patrol

and his motorbike goes ...
"Vrooom vrooom vrooom!
Vrooom vrooom vrooom!"

Here is the traffic all ground to a halt
and the policeman calls out ...

Here is the family off on their holiday
and the little girl goes ...
"Are we nearly there yet...?"

And the car goes ...

"Brrrmm brrrmm brrrmm ...
brrrmm brrrmm brrrmm..."

Here are the Duke and Duchess out for a drive
and the Duchess enquires ...
"Parker! Parker! Do see what is holding us up!"

And the Rolls Royce (very quietly) goes ...
**"Whisper whisper whisper ...
whisper whisper whisper..."**

Here is the school bus, stuck in the jam
and the school boys shout ...
"We're late! We're late! It's great! It's great!"

And the school bus goes ...
   "Chug chug chuggety chug ...
   chug chug chuggety chug..."

Here is the racing car off to the track
and its driver fumes ...
"Hurry up! I'm overheating – and so is my car!"

And the racing car goes ...

"Pop pop pop ...

bang bang, hissssss..."

Here is the ice-cream van off to the beach
and Mr Luigi cries ...
"Mamma mia! My ice-creams are melting!"

And his ice-cream van goes ...
"Ding ding ding ...
ding ding-a-ling..."

Here is the beach buggy off to the coast
and the surfers mumble ...
"Hey man! We're missing the tide..."

And their buggy goes ...

"Bumble bumble bumble ...
bumble bumble bumble..."

Here is the road sweeper spinning its brushes
and its driver chuckles ...

"Nice little rest, nice little rest..."

And the road sweeper goes ...
"Whoosh whoosh whoosh ...
whoosh whoosh whoosh..."

And here are the culprits who are causing the jam ...
Farmer Jake's prize sheep have escaped
from their field ...

And they go …
"Baaa! Baaa! Baaa!

Baaa! Baaa! Baaa…"

And here's everyone herding the sheep
back into their field and they all go ...

"Move along now, sheep! Move along!"

"Are they nearly there yet...?"

"Parker! Parker! Push the sheep! Push!"

"We're still late! It's still great!"

"Hurry up, sheep! I'm overheating!"

"Mamma mia! One of them has trodden on my foot!"

"Hey man! These sheep are heavy..."

"I *was* having a nice little rest..."

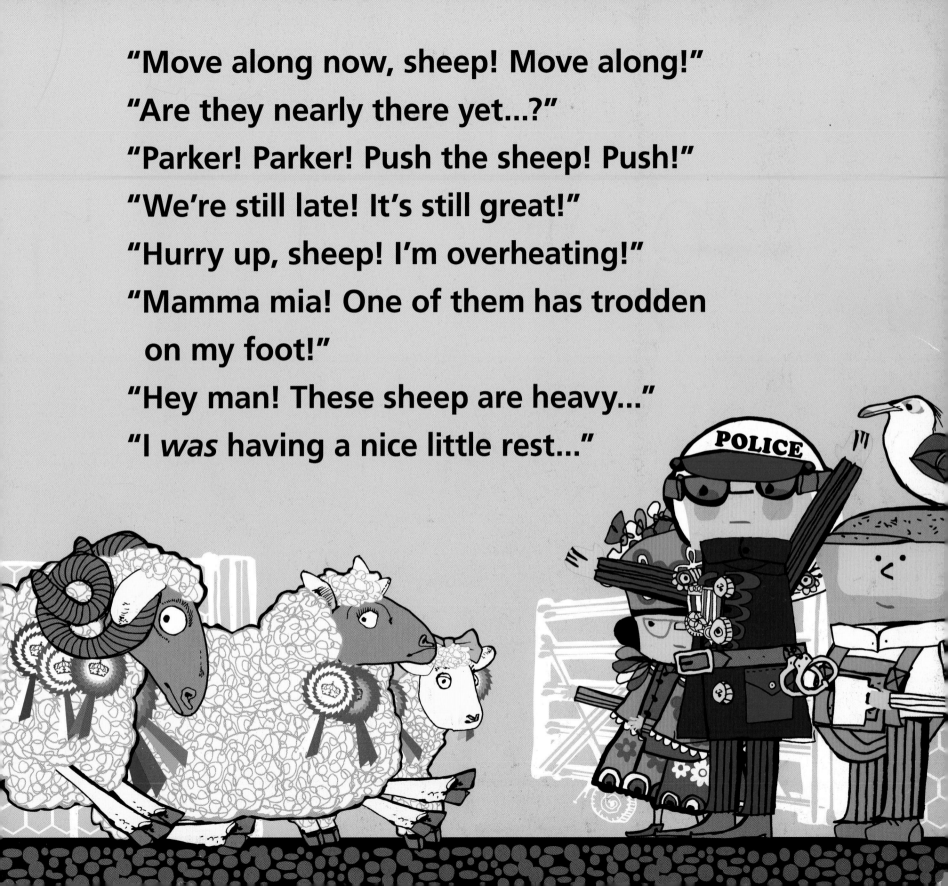

And, at last, all the cars go ...

"Whoosh, whoosh, whoosh, whoosh ...
bumble, bumble, bumble, bumble ...
ding ding, ding-a-ling ...
pop pop, bang hisss ...
chug chug, chuggety chug ...
whisper whisper, whisper whisper ...
brrrmm, brrrmm, brrrmm, brrrmm ...
woof woof woof ...

WOOF!"

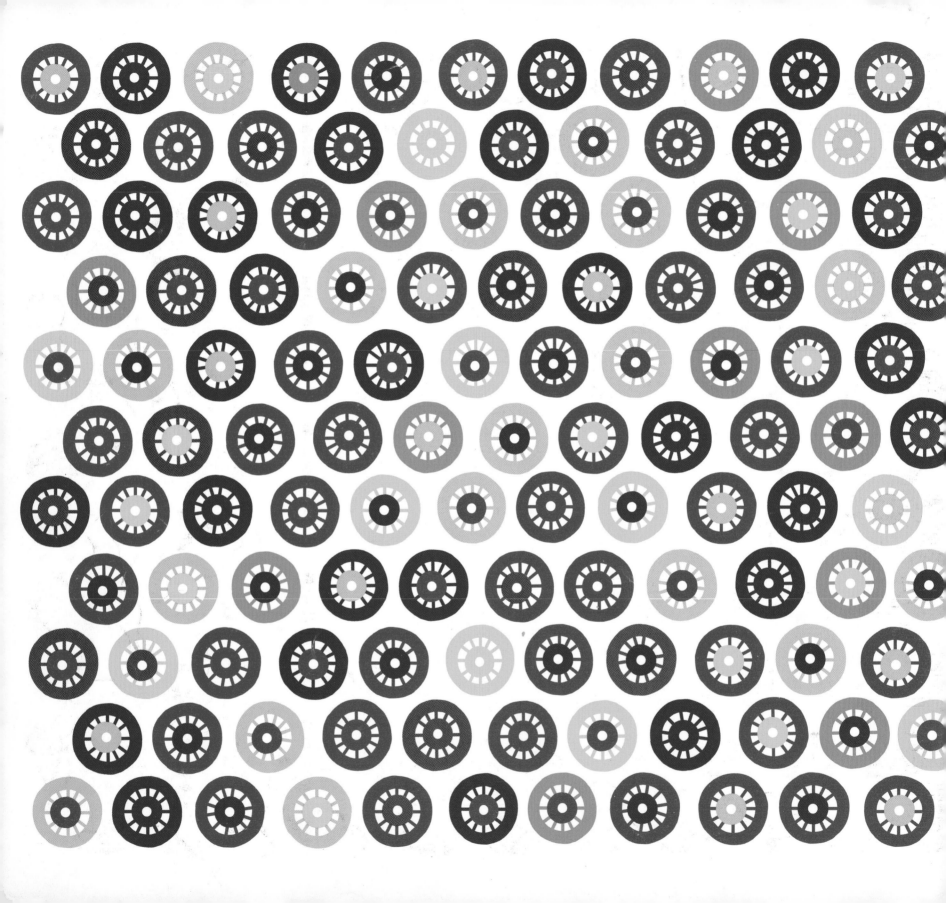

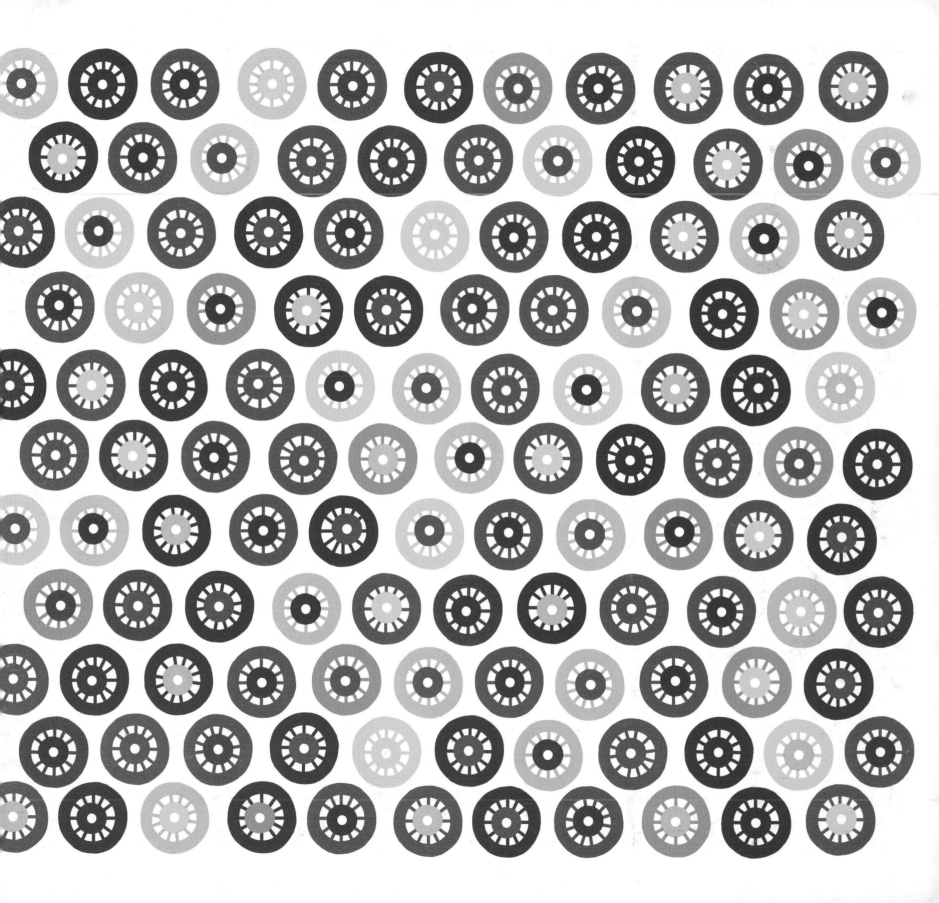

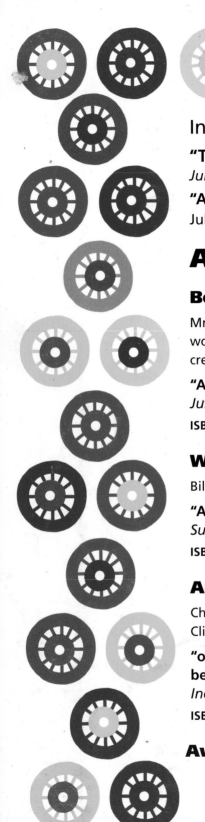

In praise of **And the Cars Go...**

"Traffic jams have never looked as good"
Junior

"An exuberantly noisy book for all those who love a racket and anything that moves!"
Julia Eccleshare, *Lovereading4kids.co.uk*

Also by William Bee...

Beware of the Frog

Mrs Collywobbles lives on the edge of a big, dark, scary wood. The only thing protecting her from all the horrible creatures that live in it is … her little pet frog.

"A great read-aloud book."
Junior

ISBN 978-1-4063-1931-6

Whatever

Billy can be very difficult to please… Whatever.

"A delightful cautionary tale."
Sunday Telegraph

ISBN 978-1-4063-0133-5

And the Train Goes...

Chuff chuff, chufferty-chuff… Puff puff, pufferty puff… Clickerty click, clickerty clack, woo wooooo…

"one of those welcome picture books that turns the bedtime story into live entertainment"
Independent

ISBN 978-1-4063-4488-2

Available from all good booksellers

www.walker.co.uk

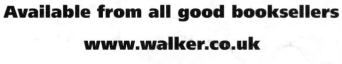